"Renaissance Men"

By

Matt Heath

For Sofia

Characters:

Raph

Mikey

The Bartender

The Bar Maid

The Bar Fly

Act 1 Scene 1

The scene opens with Michelangelo the painter sitting in a dimly lit bar. There is a bartender standing behind the bar. There is a bar maid cleaning tables. Raphael the painter enters.

Disclaimer: The author of this play is completely aware that the characters in this play would have spoken Italian and not English. The author of this play is also aware of the historical inaccuracies of this play. So for those of you willing to suspend your disbelief Grazie. As for the rest of you Vafanculo....

Raph: Ciao! Come va?

Mikey: Ahh nothin much Raph...

Raph: Why did you invite me to this bar?

Mikey: I don't know I'm depressed I guess.

Raph: Depressed!? You're the most famous artist in the world right now.

Mikey: Ahh... Vafanculo Raph. You got no idea what you're talking about. Have you seen the shit Leo has been cookin up?

Raph: Leo ain't got shit on you man. People are going to travel all the way around the world for the rest of eternity just to see your chapel.

Mikey: Don't be such a kiss culo bro. It's not helping. You know what Leo says about me and my chapel and you and Donatello for that matter.

Raph: What?

Mikey: He says we move like tortugas.

Raph: Tortugas? Turtles?

Mikey: Si. Here I am busting my marone for years to finish painting this chapel and he has the nerve to call us tortugas. My hand is crippled from working so hard. I'm like a fucking mutant.

Raph: Ohh... You are not just a mutant tortuga. Our self-portraits will keep us youthful forever. And we may be slow but we are skilled like Asian warriors. So if anything the four of us are like teenage mutant ninja tortugas.

Mikey: The paint fumes must be getting to your head man. You must be retarded if you think Michelangelo, Rapheal, Donatello and Leonardo are going to be remembered as teenage mutant ninja tortugas.

Raph: What do you think bar keep?

Bartender: I kind of like the sound of it.

Mikey: Ahh.. Vafanculo!

Raph: Oh... come on don't be like that man. You know what your problem is you need to get laid.

Mikey: That's the last thing I need Raph.

Raph: You're all wound up Mikey. I would be to if the Holy Father was on my ass to finish the damn chapel... Wait a second... He hasn't touched you? Has he Mike?

Mikey: Seriously man? Vafanculo. How could you talk about the Holy Father like that? That's why I'm painting the ceiling of the chapel and your outside painting the hall way.

Raph: Mio Dio Mike lighten up. Bartender set us up with a drink here.

The bartender puts drinks in front of them. Mikey takes a sip.

Raph: You know I also hear people talking about you being light in the loafers Mike.

Mikey spits out his drink.

Mikey: Who says that? Who says that I prefer the company of men?

Bartender: Well you're with a man right now.

Mikey: Vafanculo! You know it is true that my libido has diminished over the years. Yours would too if you were lying on your back all day painting. Lying on my back at home has become nauseating and as has sex. That's why I sleep in my armchair.

Raph: You do? You poor bastard.

Mikey: How could a man who paints such bellisima pictures of naked women be thought of in such a way?

Bartender: You paint pictures of naked men too…

Mikey: Vafanculo!

Raph: So this is why you invited me out here? To tell me about your limp dick and weird sleeping habits?

Mikey: Uhh.. No why the hell do you think I invited you out here?

Raph: Well with my whole "You're gay theory" I thought you wanted to fuck me.

Mikey: I invited you out here to tell you that I've lost my faith. I've given up. And I'm going to kill myself.

Cut to: Act 2

Act 2

Scene 1

The scene opens up with Mikey and Raph sitting at the bar. The bartender is behind the bar and the bar maid is cleaning tables.

Raph: Thinking of killing yourself!? What!?

Mikey: Shhh... not so loud.

Raph: You must be insane. The most famous man in all of Rome wants to kill himself.

Mikey: I can't take it anymore Raph the loneliness is eating me up inside.

Raph: You know you just need to hear a joke. Yes a funny joke to brighten your spirits.

Mikey: Vafanculo.

Bartender: Let's hear it!

Bar Maid: Yea let's hear it.

Raph: Okay so a bowl of pasta fagioli walks into a bar. The bartender says you look kind of depressed there pasta what's eating you? The bowl of pasta fagioli says "I'm a recovering alcoholic and I haven't had a drink in years. My wife just left me. She took the kids with her. I'm up to my eyeballs in debt. In fact I'm drowning in debt. I often think of hanging myself with a belt although it wouldn't work out that well being that I'm a bowl of soup and I don't have a neck. The reason my wife can no longer stand me is because I was in an accident involving a horse. I fell off the horse and it kicked me right in the bowl cracking it. Hot fagioli was all over the horse's culo. I was left brain damaged. Unable to work I was not able to provide for my family any more. So bartender could you please set me up with that drink?" So the bartender says to the pasta fagioli. "I'm sorry. We don't serve food here."

Mikey: That was the worst joke I've ever heard.

Bartender: Ha! We don't serve food here. That's a great one!

Bar Maid: I didn't think it was that funny.

Raph: Well I'm a painter. Not a damn stand up philosopher. What did you expect?

Mikey: Good jokes start with knock knock and the best jokes end with when he woke up he actually fucked a sheep.

Bartender: Yea I like those too.

Raph: See Mike that's your problem. You have a sick and twisted world perspective. I think that the paint fumes have gone to your head.

Mikey: I'm close to the edge Raph. Don't push me.

Raph: I'm telling you man you just need to get laid. Fuck the bar maid.

Mikey: Why?

Raph: Because she's hot.

Mikey: Well if your claim that I'm the most famous man in Rome is true then why would I fuck a common bar maid?

Bar Maid: You know I'm standing right here.

Raph: She's good in bed man, and she's easy.

Bar Maid: I can hear literally everything you're saying.

Mikey: How would you even know that about her?

Raph: I fucked her last week.

Bar Maid: Well now everybody knows.

Raph: The bartender has fucked her too.

The bartender smiles and winks at Mikey.

Mikey: I don't understand why you would think that "The great Michelangelo" would want you motherless fucks sloppy seconds.

Bar Maid: I don't know what's so great about you. The only thing you can seem to hold straight up is your paintbrush.

Bartender: Ha cuz you gotta limp dick.

Raph: Don't listen to them Mike. They don't know the kind of stress your under.

Mikey: No Raph. They are right. I was born a poor child. And I will die a poor man. There is no God. And my little Mikey isn't spreading white paint like it used to.

Raph: You got a tough job Mike. You knew it was going to be hard though. You can't give up now.

Mikey: Yes I can.

Raph: You know I was standing outside the other day smoking my pipe and you know what I saw?

Mikey: Knowing you a prostitute.

Raph: A garbage man. I watched this man load waste inside a cart and hall it away. I thought to myself... I am not a man. The man sitting next to me is not a man. The man loading the garbage into this cart with tobacco dangling from his mouth. That is a man. Only he can appreciate the true beauty of Rome. You and I, these dish rags, we can enjoy the beauty of Rome but we can never appreciate it. Only the garbage man, the man who is elbow deep in the filth and disgust and sins of the city can truly appreciate the beauty of Rome.

Mikey: So... Che Cazzo is the point?

Raph: My point is... fuck the bar maid because the angels in heaven are waiting for the garbage man, not for you.

Mikey: This hole in the ground is my favorite bar in Rome. When they see me here they yell norm! Because it is so normal for them to see me.

Bartender: No we don't.

Raph: So what Mike? I come here all the time too. I fucked the bar maid... still here.

Mikey: There's a difference between you and me man. I don't shit where I eat.

Raph: I didn't say you should take a shit on her or eat her out.

Mikey: You have difficulties understanding modern phrases don't you?

Raph: I wouldn't eat her out anyways. She's got herpes. I should know I gave it to her.

Mikey: Wow...

Bar Maid: Wow... it burns is more like it.

Bartender: You got that herpes from him! Wow I can't wait to tell people that I've contracted "The Great Raphael's Herpes."

Bar Maid: I wouldn't tell people that. He's not that great either.

Raph: Yea I don't need guys walking around saying that I gave them herpes. I'm already getting enough shit from the other painters for hanging out with Mikey here.

Mikey: What part of "I'm going to kill myself" did you not understand Raph?

Raph: Mikey... take it easy. By the end of the night you'll have your faith back. You'll embrace life. Your dick will be as hard as a coliseum stone. And God himself will be smiling down on you. Just stick with me pal.

Mikey: What makes you so sure you can help me?

Raph: Well you invited me out here didn't you? We're friends aren't we? Just have a little faith in me.

Mikey: What kind of God would make a man such a lonely creature?

Raph: Mikey. Mike! Che Cazzo man? I'm here. These slobs are here.

Bartender: I'm here.

Bar Maid: Mio Dio. I'm here. I wish I weren't.

Mikey: I'm alone in my mind. I'm alone when I paint. I'm alone in the church halls and I'm alone between the sheets.

Raph: Well everybody's got to be alone sometimes man. You know what the problem is we get bored with all this painting and shit.

Mikey: What?

Raph: Yea all this art, painting, sculptures and shit. Sure you can look at it but wouldn't you rather just sit on your culo and be entertained. I'll bet you like twenty years from now there's gonna be this guy who writes plays about love and how beautiful it can be... and tragic at the same time. We'll have plays to make us laugh and plays to make us cry. We'll have peace of mind because the plays will take our minds off the bullshit.

Mikey: Pfff... that's perfect Raph! And this great writer of yours? A Roman?

Raph: English...

Mikey: I can imagine it now. Some British insect preaching about peace and love. Hopefully no one kills him.

Raph: You're so negative. You paint all these images of heaven during the day and then drown yourself in booze at night. Go outside and get some fresh air. Walk the streets at night and you'll see heaven is a place on earth.

Mikey: Heaven does not exist.

Raph: Heaven is whatever you think it is. Whatever you picture in your mind. That's where you're going.

Mikey: How do you figure?

Raph: I'll give you an example. I used to go with this woman. She loved horses. In fact she loved horses more than people. So I asked her if she thought there were horses in heaven. She said of course. So I gave her this hypothetical situation. I said let's say you get to the golden gates and St. Peter says okay you've been a good person. You get into heaven and your horse gets into heaven too. But here's the deal... Only one of you gets a pair of wings. You or the horse what do you choose? And Mio Dio... You know what this bella said to me?

Mikey: What?

Raph: She chose the fucking horse. Can you imagine being in heaven without any wings? I guess it makes sense if you love horses and all. Fly around on the horse instead of flying yourself. Because che cazzo is she going to do if she had the wings? Is the horse gonna ride her?

Mikey: So what's your point?

Raph: My point is fuck the bar maid. Because if heaven is what you make of it you will never be alone there. Because that's what you want. So while you're here on earth just enjoy not being alone for five minutes... or three... or two. However long you last that is.

Mikey: Raph the bar maid isn't even interested in me.

Bartender: That's not true. She talks about you all the time. She even yells your name during sex.

Mikey: Really?

Raph: Yea with me too.

Mikey: I'm not interested in any cheap thrills.

Raph: Mike the whole idea of heaven is just a cheap thrill. Why do you think a guy like St. Peter is working the gate? The guy was butt ugly.

Mikey: Che cazzo are you talking about?

Raph: What I'm saying is heaven has a bouncer. Nightclubs have bouncers. Nice places have a hostess. If heaven were a nice place they'd have a belissima angel working as a hostess guiding people in. Heaven has a St. Peter though. He is a bouncer. He might not even let you in based on the shoes you're wearing.

Mikey: And your point is that I should fuck the bar maid. I get it.

Raph: No my point is that you need some new shoes.

Mikey: New shoes?

Raph: Yes comfortable footwear is the key to a happy life. I mean you have backaches all the time. You can't make use of little Mikey. I bet if you had a more comfortable pair of shoes your life would turn around.

Mikey: That can't be it.

Raph: Then you tell me "Oh Great Michelangelo." What is the key to a happy life?

Mikey: I would say that it is the way you wake up in the morning. The more natural of an awakening the happier your days on this planet will be.

Raph: And what is the most natural way to wake up?

Mikey: Why the gentle touch of your lover of course.

Raph: I whole-heartedly disagree. The most natural way to wake up is by the slap of a prostitute's mano. Only after you pay her the shillings you owe her do you have peace of mind and are therefore in a more natural state.

Mikey: I highly doubt that is the most natural way to wake up in the morning.

Raph: What do you think barkeep?

Bartender: With all do respect I think that you're both wrong. The most natural way to wake up is the sound of a rooster crowing. When you whistle a bird might whistle back. Parrots can even repeat what you say. But when the rooster sleeps he can hear all the moans and aches of the people around him. And then when the rooster wakes up from its final nightmare it lets out a crow.

Mikey: I think you may be wiser than you lead on to be bartender. For that is the most natural way to wake up.

Raph: So there it is Mike. We just have to get you a rooster.

Mikey: The problem is I can't sleep until I finish the chapel and I won't sleep.

Raph: You know Mike you knew what you were getting into when you decided to take this job.

Mikey: Well it is a little more complicated than that. When the Holy Father asked me if I wanted to paint the Sistine Chapel I thought he had asked me to paint sixteen chapels. When he told me that it was only one I agreed. I had no idea how big the damn place was though.

Raph: If anyone can do it, it has got to be you man. Think of yourself as David and the chapel as Goliath. Your trusty slingshot is your paintbrush.

Mikey: I had already thought of the statue of David as Goliath and myself as David. My chisel was my slingshot.

Raph: So do it again. You can do it man. I believe in you.

Mikey: Such a kiss culo man. You and that painting of Leo and me depicted as gods. And you got yourself tucked away way in the corner. Why? What makes me so much better then you?

Raph: You're my hero. Everything I do is merely a copy off of you.

Mikey: Do you mean that?

Raph: I have this vision in my mind Mike. I can see people traveling all the way across the world to wait in line for hours upon hours just to get a glimpse at your work. This chapel that is making you lose your faith will do the opposite for people who have lost there's.

Mikey: I highly doubt that.

Bartender: They will wait for hours you say?

Raph: Yes in fact we will capitalize on this too. People waiting in line will pay a small fee. While others who pay more will be able to skip the line and see the church right away.

Bartender: What an amazing idea. What do you call it?

Raph: Fast pass.

Bartender: Wow... fast pass.

Mikey: We cannot do that.

Raph: Why not?

Mikey: Tis unethical. The Holy Father would never allow it.

Bartender: Ehh I guess your right who would cut in line to see a church?

Mikey: Can you not see how wrong that is Raph?

Raph: Think about how much money we could make? People will pay months worth of food just to see your paintings a little bit faster.

Mikey: This is a church were talking about. I suppose when I die all I have to do is slip St. Peter a few shillings to get out of purgatory faster and I'll get right to the front of the pearly gates.

Raph: Well now you just sound ridiculous.

Bartender: I agree how could shillings be the currency in heaven? They use angel bucks.

Mikey/Raph: Angel bucks?

Bartender: Si.

Mikey: Well I don't think the Holy Father ever mentioned a currency in heaven.

Raph: Well how do you suppose you pay for things...With God's love?

Mikey: Well actually yes.

Bar Maid: Che fucking cazzo? There is no currency in heaven. You just get whatever you wish for.

Raph: Well I wish for you to roll in the hay with my friend Mikey here.

Bar Maid: You're barking up the wrong tree.

Raph: What does the bark of a tree have to do with anything?

Mikey: Oh Marone... You fucking idiot. It's a metaphor. Being that she is a bird and you are a dog that is barking up the wrong tree.

Raph: It's funny I have heard that expression before many times but have never understood it.

Mikey: Your stupidity never ceases to surprise me, but back to the fact of the matter, you can't let people skip in line to make a profit. You'll end up being first in line for hell.

Raph: If you think for a second that we don't live in corrupt city your crazy.

Mikey: The city may be corrupt but the church isn't.

Raph: Oh yea the church that hired just one guy to paint a whole church causing him to lose his manhood, faith and will to live. That church isn't corrupt? Admit it Mike your full of shit you're not going to kill yourself.

Mikey: I promise you tonight is my last night on earth. I cannot paint another stroke.

Raph: I keep telling you Mike it's not that kind of stroke that's your problem, but if you still love the church so much maybe you should go to the Holy Father for some guidance.

Mikey: I could never let him know that "The Great Michelangelo" has lost his faith.

Raph: That's your other problem man. How could someone who wants to kill himself have such a big ego? How could someone who has no faith in God have faith in the church? You are a walking contradiction.

Mikey: I may have lost my faith but the Roman Catholic Church will always be my home.

Raph: Man you're ass backwards. No one goes to church if they don't believe in God. In fact most people have it the other way around. They believe in God and don't go to church.

Mikey: We live in Rome. Everyone goes to church.

Bartender: I don't go to church.

Raph: But you believe in God?

Bartender: Si.

Mikey: Well why don't you go to church then?

Bartender: I don't know mass can be boring sometimes.

Raph: He's right.

Mikey: Well I suppose the Holy Father could spice things up every once in a while.

Bartender: Same prayers, same hymns, same Bible.

Raph: What about you sweetheart? You go to church?

Bar Maid: Not even once.

Raph: See Mikey? You believe in God though right?

Bar Maid: Of course.

Raph: I was right again Mikey. You're like the guy that runs the carmella shop. Of course you stopped liking carmella. You've had too much of a good thing. Anyways all this talk about religion is making me have to take a shit.

Raph exits. The Bar Maid starts cleaning up after Raph.

Mikey: You know I'm nothing like him.

Bar Maid: I know I just don't understand how you can hang out with a guy like him.

Mikey: Well he can really be quite insightful at times. Well...when he's not thinking about sex or booze at least.

Bar Maid: Well I don't think he's going to convince you to finish the chapel.

Mikey: I don't know he's certainly got my mind off things. He's a friend that can make you laugh when things get rough. He's true blue. One time he even pushed my horse carriage out of the mud in the middle of the night. That's a true friend.

Bar Maid: I wouldn't know I don't have a horse carriage.

Mikey: Of course. How rude of me. A common bar maid like yourself has to walk everywhere and here I am with my rich white people problems.

Bar Maid: First of all you're not rich. I know all about you "Great Michelangelo." And you may be famous but you're certainly not rich. Second of all I don't walk. I have a horse.

Mikey: A bar maid with a horse? Wow... I don't think there's anything more attractive than a chick riding a horse to a bar.

Bar Maid: Well my horse is the only thing that I truly love.

Mikey: Wait, you are the girl Raph was talking about. The one who would choose a horse having wings in heaven over herself?

Bar Maid: That's me.

Mikey: That is an interesting theory you have about heaven. But aren't you worried you're going to hell if you've never been to church?

Bar Maid: I'm waiting for the right church?

Mikey: What do you mean by that?

Bar Maid: It hasn't finished being painted yet.

Mikey: Ohh...

Bar Maid: You know I would go to church I just have a tough time with all the things the Bible says and what you guys say for that matter.

Mikey: What did we say?

Bar Maid: All that stuff about St. Peter and the pearly gates. It's all bullshit. Heaven isn't a place where people are living together. You're not going to meet your dead relatives. Your mind is just going to be finally at peace. You will finally be at rest at the bosom of the Lord.

Mikey: That's a beautiful thought. Don't tell Raph that though. He laughs every time h hears the word bosom.

Bar Maid: God I hate him.

Mikey: Why did you sleep with him anyway?

Bar Maid: Well I have a thing for painters and I guess I thought I could get closer to you.

Mikey: Why would you want to get closer to me? You don't even think I could finish the Chapel.

Bar Maid: I never said you couldn't finish the chapel. I said that Raph couldn't help you finish the chapel.

Mikey: Well than who can?

Bar Maid: Well what you need is a muse an inspiration of some kind.

Mikey: Inspiration? I suppose you're right but from where?

Mikey finishes his drink.

Bar Maid: Well I'll tell you one thing. You're not going to find it at the bottom of a cup.

The Bar Maid grabs Mikey's arm.

Mikey: Where from then?

Bar Maid: What do you find beautiful?

Mikey: The moon I suppose.

Bar Maid: And what is it that you like about the moon?

Mikey: Well to me the moon is quite a mysterious place. If all it is, is just a giant rock why does it have such a heavenly glow?

Bar Maid: I don't really know.

Mikey: And you know on certain nights you can even see a certain glow that surrounds the moon.

Bar Maid: I suppose it does. Your eyes are immediately drawn to it.

Mikey: It's not so different from you. You know?

Bar Maid: What?

Mikey: You have a certain glow about you an aura that surrounds you. It's really quite belissima.

Bar Maid: Mio Dio

Mikey: I wish I could put it in a bottle and sell it on the streets of Venezia, so I could watch lovers sit in boats and drift like lanterns through the city.

The Bar Maid and Mikey start leaning in closer and closer to each other as if they are about to kiss. Raph enters.

Raph: Listen I would not go in there for about thirty-five to forty-five minutes.

Mikey: Mio Dio Raph.

Raph: Mikey there is no point in committing suicide tonight because something just died in there.

Mikey: Must you be so revolting?

Raph: What it wasn't even me? I think a horse got in the bathroom somehow. Anyways. What were we talking about?

Mikey: I believe you were trying to reinstall my faith by telling me how corrupt the church is.

Raph: It's not just the church that's corrupt it's the whole world, this city in particular.

Mikey: Well all city living is the same. It can't be changed.

Raph: Well if the church is so great and powerful in Rome how come the Holy Father rides in on a gilded carriage while people are begging in the streets?

Mikey: Well the Holy Father is not God himself. He can't fix everything.

Bartender: Some men hustle some men beg.

Mikey: And who are you to point fingers on who's morally corrupt? Where would you be this evening if I didn't invite you out here? Some lupanarium like every other evening letting the she wolves feast upon you.

Raph: Well who are you to judge me now? You're the one talking about killing yourself. Maybe you should try my way of life for a change because you know something Mike? I don't want to end mine. I embrace it.

Mikey: As famous as we are why on earth do you need to pay for sex?

Raph: This is where you cease to understand " Oh Great Michelangelo." I don't pay for sex I pay for them to leave. The level of fame we achieved has too much power. I'm at the point where I just pretend normal women don't exist because they have a distorted image of me. It's even worse for you for that matter. They see Michelangelo and Rapheal the artists, the legends the Gods among men. They don't see what pathetic shlubs we really are. So my advice to you is; either hit it and quit it with no emotional attachments, or go the other route, and just get a whore every night like I do.

Mikey: I'm speechless.

Raph: No one ever said fame was going to be easy.

Mikey: I never asked for fame.

Raph: Well what is it that you want then?

Mikey: I want to be in love.

Raph: God you are fucking annoying.

Mikey What?

Raph: You remind me of the man that has no arms who sits outside the Sistine Chapel waiting for spare shillings. I give this man shillings every day. Every day he sits there in the same spot. I give and I give and I give and do things ever get any better for this man? Of course not. I feel bad the man has no arms. He'll never know the joy of painting like we do. He'll never able to feel the warm cheek of his lover with the palm of his hand. I give to this man every day but now I will stop. You just made me realize that it's only when you stop giving that the armless man will find a new spot to be. And maybe just maybe he'll be happier where ever he goes.

Mikey: Vafanculo Raph! You almost had me there for a second, before I realized that the whole point to your ridiculous parable was for me to join you at the lupanarium for a night with a she wolf. And by accompanying you, you will feel better about your own shitty existence.

Raph: Mikey the world is changing. Do you really think this age of art and beauty were living in is going to last forever? For the first time ever us the creative types are the ones who hold the cards.

How long is it going to be before some vicious tyrant comes along and knocks us off this pedestal we were put on. Huh you tell me?

Bartender: I don't mean to bud in but "The Great Rapheal " is right sir. You should be happy.

Mikey: I am grateful for the time we live in. Art and beauty are held in the highest regard and for that I am thankful, but the amount of pressure that is pushing down on me is too much for me to handle.

Bartender: The lord asks us to move mountains but only asks us to carry a shovel.

Raph: Go back to wiping bar sweat. Mikey is a painter not a digger you fool. I'll tell you what's up Mikey it's like this. The chapel is your life's work. You might die alone crippled and poor but you'll be seen as a legend. Living now maybe a struggle for you but look how happy your making everyone else. And think about how shitty it's going to be in the future. I believe that one day they are going to have machines on top of wheels that will take people place to place at high speeds. Flying machines will take you all over the world and there will be machines where I can see you and talk to you even though you're hundreds of miles away.

Mikey: That sounds amazing.

Raph: No Mikey, it will be terrible. Imagine people using these machines on wheels and your horse being a domestic pet. It will have no use. It will run around the back yard with no freedom to take you from town to town. It will live a depressed boxed in life and die depressed and obsolete.

Bartender: What does a horse's happiness have to do with ours though?

The bar maid stomps on the bartenders foot.

Bartender: Owww!!

Raph: Well us as human beings will be depressed and obsolete as well. We'll have machines to do everything for us. People will be glued to screens illuminating light and drool like zombies staring at lives that they could have. It will be a miserable life indeed.

Mikey: Raph how do you know all this?

Raph: Leo tells me of his nightmares quite often. Anyways I need to smoke you?

Mikey: No I'm good.

Raph: Barkeep?

Bartender: Yea sure.

The bartender and Raph exit.

Cut to: Act 2 Scene 2

Act 2

Scene 2

The scene opens with Michelangelo sitting at the bar. The Bar Maid sits down next to him.

Bar Maid: You don't think that he really means all that stuff about the future do you?

Mikey: Well if it comes from Leo it must be true. He's a pretty smart guy. I wouldn't worry though. We're all just pawns in this chess game of life anyways. Life sucks now. Life will suck again later. No difference.

Bar Maid: No I mean what he said about horses. Do you think it's true?

Mikey: Wow... I wish I loved anything as much as you love horses.

Bar Maid: You love to paint don't you?

Mikey: Art... beauty. These are just concepts...ideas. You actually love something tangible, something real.

Bar Maid: Your statue of David, I remember the first time I ever saw it. I thought it was the most beautiful thing that I've ever seen. That is real and the chapel is real too.

Mikey: It won't be if it's never finished.

Bar Maid: I'm telling you all you need is some inspiration. All you need to do is look inside yourself.

Mikey: I look inside myself and there's nothing there. You spoke of a muse but there is no such thing. I thought my wife was my muse but she has abandoned me because of my obsession with my work. I tried telling her time and time again that it was all for her.

Bar Maid: Maybe a muse isn't one person in particular. Maybe it's how a person can make you feel.

Mikey: You know there is something about how you look at me that makes me feel innocent like a child and confident like a man all at the same time.

Bar Maid: You have such a way with words. I wish I could say something to make you feel as good as you just made me feel.

Mikey: When the chapel opens... if it ever opens. I want you to look up. You'll see an angel in your image. Because that's what you are you're an angel.

Bar Maid: Can the angel have a horse?

Mikey: Angels have wings sweetheart. They don't have horses.

Bar Maid: That's still the most romantic thing I've ever heard.

Mikey: If only I could paint with words.

Bar Maid: Well if you're going to do that for me can I at least cook you dinner?

Mikey: Yea sure.

Bar Maid: You like chicken?

Mikey: Si.

Cut to: Act 2 Scene 3.

Act 2

Scene 3

Michelangelo is sitting at the bar. Raphael and the bartender enter. They are followed by a

homeless man (known as the Bar Fly)

Mikey: Oh man... Not this guy again.

Raph: Mikey! You remember old Sprinkles don't you?

Mikey: Sprinkles? Is that a name? Is that even a thing?

The bar fly starts scratching himself.

Mikey: Bartender can you please get this guy out of here.

Bartender: I think he's funny.

Raph: Oh come on Mike let him stay.

Mikey: He can't even afford a drink. He's loitering for God's sake.

Raph: Well we can't all be famous artists Mike. I mean he's not bothering anybody it's just us here.

The bar fly belches loudly.

Mikey: I suppose your right.

Raph: Weewww!!! Sprinkles!!

Bar Fly: Ahhh!!! Who are you people?

Mikey: Mister uhhh... Sprinkles... We're artists. We're friends.

Bar Fly: My names not Sprinkles!! Slurp in terf in cats chew pop cough...nnnn mmmmm formaggio.. fantasma.. cats mmm tomp tomp tomp.

Raph: Well what is your name then?

Bar Fly: The end is near! Rats rats oooops nnnn fazitche cazo wimpisite yackin kim kardashian.

Mikey: Uhh.. Raph?

Raph: It's all right Mikey. What do you mean the end is near?

Bar Fly: End of the world. The new world is the end of the world. And rats and cats and R.E.M. songs about I n life n space and L. Ron Travolta.

Raph: What the fuck is he talking about?

Mikey: I don't know but he's scaring me.

Raph: I think we should buy him a drink.

Mikey: Are you fucking kidding me Raph? I think the guy has had enough to drink.

The bar fly starts urinating in the corner.

Raph: Alcoholics have a certain amount of wisdom to them. This guy could be the answer to all your problems.

Bartender: Hey put your dick away!

The bar fly stops peeing puts himself away and sits down at the bar.

Raph: Set this man up with a drink bar keep and the rest of us for that matter.

Mikey: If you buy him a drink he'll never leave.

Raph: I'd like you to take a look at this man Mikey.

The bartender sets the three men up with drinks. The bar fly immediately starts chugging his.

Raph: You see, alcoholics live without fear.

Mikey: What do you mean by that?

Raph: A sober person lives with many fears. They are afraid of things that go bump in the night. When you're an alcoholic you are the thing that goes bump in the night.

The Bar Fly starts pounding down on the bar.

Bar Fly: Ahhh! Ahhh! Ahhhh!!!!

The bar maid enters from the back.

Bar Maid: Che Cazzo is going on out here?

Mikey: Raph wanted to buy this homeless guy a drink and now he's going nuts I guess.

Raph: Relax! He just wants another one. Set him up bar keep.

Bartender: I don't think I should sir.

Mikey: See Raph. He's not wanted here.

Bar Maid: Well actually I'd choose the bar fly over Raph any day.

Raph: He's a struggling artist unwanted by the rest of society just like us Mike.

Mikey: He's wasted.

Raph: He's fine. Bar fly what year is it?

Bar Fly: Fifteen..not...teen...teen blarven.

Raph: That was damn close.

Mikey: What country do we live in?

Bar Fly: A country that will one day be most known for... mmmm... nnnn.. moving pictures... of gangsters... mmmm a bloody head of a horse in a mans bed.

Bar Maid: Mio Dio that's terrible.

Mikey: That's it! He's scaring her Raph.

Raph: What the hell are moving pictures?

The bar maid starts crying.

Mikey: Get the hell out of here!

The Bar Maid runs into the back. Mikey pulls the Bar Fly off his bar stool and tosses him out.

Raph: Jesus tap dancing Christ!

Mikey: I don't know what tap dancing is but stop taking the lords name in vain.

Raph: Stop getting all worked up Mike. I think that Jesus has a sense of humor.

Mikey: No he doesn't.

Raph: How do you know?

Mikey: He never told any jokes in the Bible.

Raph: Well what's the deal with the Bible anyhow?

Mikey: Che cazzo are you talking about?

Raph: Well did you ever notice that it was only Jesus' buddies that ever wrote about him? How come there's nothing autobiographic? Who knows maybe he didn't know how to write or read? I mean look Jesus might have performed some miracles and all but maybe he was as illiterate as fuck.

Mikey: That's blasphemy Raph.

Raph: How come there is no book of Joseph for that matter? What was his deal? His would have been the most interesting too. A real page-turner.

Dear Diary,

 A supernatural being knocked up my wife. I don't know if I believe her but she scares me.

Mikey: It was never really Joseph I had a problem with in the Bible. It was Mary.

Raph: Well everyone has a tough time excepting that Mary was a virgin.

Mikey: Well that's a leap of faith that everyone who is a Catholic must except. I just don't like how the end of the new testament plays out.

Raph: Well no one wants Jesus to be crucified but he died for our sins you know?

Mikey: No… no hear me out. I don't like how Jesus had his mother with him throughout his whole life. Even right up until the end. It was no wonder he was able to preach about doing good for others. His mother was pure. She watched over him every step of the way too. It's easy to help others when you constantly have your mother around. She was always there to wash his clothes, cook his meals, tidy up after him. If you had the perfect mother it would be easy to be the perfect son.

Raph: My mother was a prostitute.

Mikey: That answers a lot of questions.

Raph: How bout you barkeep you got a good mother?

Bartender: I love my mama. Taught me everything I know about the art of tending bar.

Mikey: Well my mother died when I was very young. I guess I could never relate to Jesus because of it.

Raph: I guess that's why all your best work comes from the Old Testament.

Mikey: I guess so...

Raph: What was your mother's name anyway?

Mikey: Mary.

Raph: Oh shit that's cosmic.

Bartender: Your family must have been pretty religious huh?

Raph and Mikey both just stare at the Bartender for a moment.

Raph: You know being the son of someone that has the same name as the mother of our lord carries a strange burden. You aspire to be like Jesus every day. You slave away painting a church just to serve him. But you can never be Jesus Mike. You're a sinner just like me. You drink, you swear and you lust for women just like me. Like I've told you a thousand times lighten up. I'm sure that the Virgin Mary sits in a special place in heaven and there is a big table with women that share her name. It's like a special club.

Mikey: Oh come on. I'm not that much of a sinner. I'm relatively a model citizen.

Raph: Come on Mikey. You may not be a commandment breaker but you commit all seven deadly sins before you even leave your place in the morning.

Mikey: Ah Vafanculo!

Raph: You do. You wake up going "Man I can't believe my ex is fucking that guy. I'm so much better than he is." That's wrath, envy, lust and pride all right there.

Mikey: What about the other three?

Raph: "Hey I'm eating the last loaf of bread. I don't feel like stopping any where." Gluttony, greed and sloth all right there.

Mikey: Shit your right. That is how my mornings usually play out.

Raph: Don't be so hard on yourself. Like I said we're all sinners. How do you feel?

Mikey: Like shit still. I'm going to hang myself tonight and that's all there is to it.

Raph gets off his bar stool.

Raph: Well I've tried my best. I'm going to the lupanarium now. I think you should join me.

Mikey: Meaningless sex is not the answer Raph. I don't know what is.

Raph: I guess you'd rather kill yourself. I thought we had fun together tonight Mikey. We talked religion, we talked chicks. I paid a homeless guy three shillings to come in here to take a wizz to make you laugh and you just shit all over me. I don't know what's going to save you Mike but it's not going to be me. All I can tell you to do is look deep within yourself and ask.. Do I really want to die?... or do I want to fuck the bar maid?

The bar maid walks in from the back with a plate of food. Mikey does not notice.

Mikey: I told you Raph I don't shit where I eat.

Raph: Che sciffo man! I'm of here Mike! Arrivederci.

Raph exits.

Cut To: Act 2 Scene 4

The scene opens with Mikey sitting at the bar. The bartender is behind the bar. The bar maid sits

next to Mikey and hands him the plate of food.

Bar Maid: So what is that supposed to mean? You don't shit where you eat?

Mikey: Well it's just an expression. Me and Raph were just...

Bar Maid: Well my horse shits where he eats all the time. It's really quite frustrating, because not

only do I have to pick up his shit. I gotta pick up the shitty hay he doesn't eat.

Mikey: Well literally I understand you. Metaphorically I'm lost.

Bar Maid: There is no metaphor. I'm just talking horse problems here.

Mikey: Well... okay.

Bartender: I'm gonna leave... Can you close up?

Bar Maid: Certo.

Bartender: Cool... I got a horse joke for you by the way.

Bar Maid: What is It?

Bartender: What do gay horses say?

Bar Maid: What?

Bartender: Hay-yayyy!

Silence.

Bartender: Well anyways… Have fun you two.

The bartender exits.

Mikey: And you actually slept with that guy?

Bar Maid: Well you can't put the shit back in the donkey now can you?

Mikey: I would have loved to have seen Raph's reaction to that one.

Bar Maid: Well I've told that one before and he just stared at me blankly and said "no… no you can't."

Mikey: That's funny. One time Raph told me that I should sleep with this girl at the chapel that helps out with the paint. When I told him that I don't stick my quill into company ink he replied tha I was being racist.

The Bar Maid laughs.

Bar Maid: Wow…what a fucking idiot? Hey come on? The food I made you is getting cold.

Mikey: Oh I'm sorry. It looks amazing. I'll try it.

Mikey tries the food.

Mikey: Oh Mio Dio. This is fucking amazing.

Takes another bight.

Mikey: Mmmmm Mio fucking Dio! There is a stairway to heaven and it's located somewhere in Rome. That's how you got the recipe right?

Bar Maid: Prego.

Mikey: Seriously this is the best food I've ever eaten. After years of alcoholism it's like my taste buds have laid dormant for decades. This sauce has awakened them for the first time in ages. I can smell again. Mio Dio I can smell again!

Mikey keeps eating.

Bar Maid: Your being ridiculous now.

Mikey: I know soldiers that would stab a man just to get ahead in line to get a plate of this.

Bar Maid: You know what your right it is that good.

Mikey: Grazie so much!

Mikey quickly finishes the plate of food. He takes the Bar Maid by the hand and kisses her on the cheek.

Mikey: You know I don't mean to go blue but I think this food has got the blood flowing to little Mikey again.

Bar Maid: You're sure it's the food?

Mikey: Well whatever it is it's working.

Bar Maid: I guess you could call it a miracle.

Mikey: Hardly, if you could get me to paint again that would be a miracle.

Bar Maid: You know I never used to believe in miracles or the afterlife or anything like that.

Mikey: Well what happened?

Bar Maid: Well I had this friend that used to ride horses and he died. And after he died I got this strange feeling in the pit of my stomach. And it wouldn't go away for months. Then one day in the dead of winter when my horse was young it got lost in the mountains. It was not safe to go searching for the horse. And this particular mountain was known for horses falling off the side to their deaths. So all I could do was wait. Then one day the horse came back on its own and that strange feeling in my stomach went away.

Mikey: You believe your friend saved your horse.

Bar Maid: I think so.

Mikey: Well then I suppose one doesn't need wings to ride a horse in the afterlife.

Bar Maid: I guess not.

Mikey: It's funny.

Bar Maid: What's funny?

Mikey: The idea of a horse in heaven. I don't understand how an animal that is so majestic can poop so much. If being in heaven is doing what you love the most then a horse's idea of heaven would just be shitting all day. I suppose someone would have to clean it up too.

Bar Maid: I suppose horses would just shit clouds in heaven and they would just disappear.

Mikey: Well you know have in common with the horses.

Bar Maid: What?

Mikey: You're both beautiful, majestic, and I don't understand how you both have those big beautiful brown eyes.

Bar Maid: That's very nice of you.

Mikey: That is as opposed to me. I have more in common with a pile of horse shit. My spirit has gone sour. My soul attracts flies.

Bar Maid: You're wrong maybe your soul attracts flies because it is so sweet.

Mikey: Well you are sweet for saying that but I somehow still feel lonely.

Bar Maid: Michelangelo how can you be lonely? You have so much love in your heart. You release it into your artwork so beautifully. All of Rome adores you and applauds you. You are merely alone because you isolate yourself within your work. You have to let love out into the world as well as let love in. You have to let the love lift you, not only to the ceiling of the Sistine Chapel, but higher and higher until you're so close to God himself so that you can reach out and touch. And once you have touched the hand of God you will get a glimpse of the kingdom of heaven and finally know that you were never alone and you'll never be alone.

Mikey: Mio Dio. That's it!

Cut To: Act 3

Act 3

Scene 1

Mikey and the Bar Maid are both standing at the bar. Mikey leaps for joy. He embraces the Bar Maid and kisses her on the lips.

Mikey: That's it! You've saved my life. You've saved the chapel.

Bar Maid: How did I do that?

Mikey: What you just said.... that is how I'm going to finish the chapel. Rome's love lifting me will be God's love lifting Adam. Adam will reach out and touch God's hand and he will get a glimpse of the kingdom of heaven. It's beautiful.

Bar Maid: I don't understand how one image can completely change your mind.

Mikey: It's not just one image. It will be the most iconic image of the whole chapel. It will pull the whole room together. It will make sinners see the light. It will give faith to the faithless. It will be a masterpiece. I cannot thank you enough for this. I owe my life to you and I don't even know your name.

Bar Maid: It's Mary.